A Portrait of A Disordered Mind

A Portrait of A Disordered Mind

Tellwell Talent
www.tellwell.ca

ISBN
978-0-2288-6317-5 (Paperback)

For the troubled ones

Preface

This book started as a project to keep my mind sane. The idea came to me during the February of 2020, a period when my mental health was deteriorating at an exponential pace. Suffering from mental health issues my entire life, it should not have been as difficult as that period was. The book deals with all the different aspects of mental health issues I had dealt with and have to deal with on a daily basis. These are elaborated using logic and sanity defying structures that could be termed kaons or poems, but it would not matter. The book must be like this and not even a bit different if it has to represent me. But the project ended up becoming something far more significant than it was projected to be. This book is not just a rant or a cry for help; if anything, it has been written in a format to inspire the creative and rebellious nature within ourselves. Culture and language challenging sentences are sewed into each kaon to germinate interpretations. In its essence, this book is what you want it to be, and even though the project did not start like that-- it started just to help me cope with my mental state-- it became a somewhat subconscious effect of itself.

So how to read this book? The proper way would be to breeze through each chapter as they are ordered. Then, go to the different branches mentioned in any particular chapter to attain a complete picture of that chapter. In the end, the book has several themes in its essence. But one theme is not presented in the chapters and would have to be looked further to appreciate. Hopefully, it will be an interesting experience. Have fun reading.

Until

All they care about; the thoughts-- the significance of being. In desperation, the words we say are not the words we want to say. They can hear you, when your eyes flinch. They can hear you; whenever you nod your head or lick your lips to lie. They can hear you. The way you cross your arms or fold your legs; your cheeks are uplifted to project a sanguine smile even when your eyes stay barren-- they can hear you. They can hear you, and yet-- they don't.

As you read this in your head, think about the times you had to laugh even when you so desperately wanted to cry. Do you remember?

When was that?

Can you hear yourself?

Can you hear it?

The scream.

As you get quarantined in the chaos of your own doing, you lose the glitter of your eyes like the leaves of fall. And as you are falling into the depths of the hole in your chest, all you can hear are the screams. The screams-- of your past, your present, and your future. And just like Bach's never-ending canon, the melody of your heart's unfulfilled desires conquers you completely. "Is it pain?" they ask.

But you know that it's something worse. It is uncertainty. A lost parasite who found solace in your darkness; now feeds off this stern anxiety of yours. You deny it. You fight it. You beg it to go away.

Until one day-- you feel okay. A year has passed, or just a month, or just a week. But it's okay. You are okay. You wake up to a beautiful sunrise. A moment of peace sets in as the reddish glare of the sun brightens your mood. So, why were you sad at all?

They hurt you

Betrayed you

Sabotaged you

Lied to you

You forgave them.

You made sure that you set yourself apart from them. You know that we cannot experience sunrise without sunset, spring without fall, or a new book until and unless we have given up the old one. Donated to a library. Just living with the reason, for a reason-- that you and I once read those words, and those words were beautiful.

Every single line that we skimmed or read, thoroughly remembered, has ended now. We once belonged to the sonnets or the paragraphs of the book, but now it stays in distant memory, and we let go of everything as the first ray of the sun falls on the pages of our book. Peace sets in.

They try. They try to be the hope, the love, the trust that you once lost. They smile with your smile and cry with your tears. The book you donated was burnt to ashes as the library crumbled down in your anger upon yourself. "What's wrong?" they ask with a refreshing smile as a childish attempt to be the saviour of your internal demise. How will you tell them that you just cannot let go of those memories? You are suffocating yourself.

Drowning. In your pain. Does your heart bleed? Does it hurt to know that the book you once read, and lived your life through, was just filled with lies? It was just a book, just like this one.

"What's wrong?" you see their lips moving, but the sound never reaches your drums. Or maybe it does, but it gets dissolved into the noise. The negative thoughts echo from one ear to the other in your head; till they amplify into being pure hatred. Hatred of self. All selves.

Why does it not stop beating?

The heart.

It goes on and on... Like a mundane routine. Like Poseidon of Kafka, it does not care about me. Or else, it would have stopped beating on my soul.

People's voices are annoying. The silence, terrifying. "What's wrong?" they keep on asking… But you are trapped in your thoughts. You want to run away. You look outside the window and feel the refreshing breeze of Easter on your face. The coldness you feel on your nose is balanced by the stroke of noon. The sun is at its prime; his rays reflected from the dews resting on freshly sprinkled grass. The yellow-tinted-scape is lifelike. Your lungs filled with cheerfulness and bliss. But the moment you turn back, the lungs deflate; the stomach is occupied by misery. "What's wrong?" you want to yell- "There is not enough blood around me."

People spend their lives searching for something that can provide them eternal happiness, whether money, desires, or an imaginary friend, but they ignore that true contentment is an ever-changing manifold of events, small events, which sums up to provide you lifelong joy. You know that. Everyone knows that. Yet choose to ignore the indifference of their existence. And before you can fully understand what's wrong with you, the sun sets. You crawl up in your bed, and you wait until sunrise.

Blue

Which is bluer?

Cold.

Lonely.

Sad.

Hungry.

Blue.

Negative.

Or

Hope.

Sam

Sam was a little girl who wasn't obsessed with the beauty of this sad world.

She laughed and loved her friends.

She was in love with this pleasure-- sitting under this beautiful tree.

It was green, red, and blue.

Sam could feel it.

She felt the tree.

She felt life in the tree.

She felt darkness in that life.

But the innocence inside her changed that darkness-- and the tree was no longer white.

Every passing second, the tree and Sam bonded, the sky turned pinker than witnessable.

Sam felt safe-- the tree comforted her.

They could see their future together.

Sam was a little girl at the moment-- but with the tree, she felt like a woman.

The passion brightened each cell of her body. The colours transformed into sounds, and among those sounds--was the peace that we can never experience--not until we inject ourselves too.

Ego

Such a delphic phrase of origin

Brightens the folie...

Spoken by the wise, caressed by Athena's fingers. Wisdom is a boon, ego a bane.

Lose it and become a better man.

But will somebody tell me, will somebody whisper in my shut ears

Why should I?

Why shouldn't I tame all the horses and leave the carriages behind?

Why shouldn't I blow the hot-blazing glass until it cools down?

Or just break it on my face, let the blood from my face stain the core of my identity.

I can, cause I earned it.

So, I won't, cause I earned it.

Chapter

This chapter started as an attempt to explain the fallen circumstances of the manipulative mind. But like the squeezing void of light's half-life, the attempt is futile, non-eventual and, delphic. To capture the war between the self and the loathing, the ego and the loving, we need to take a journey through the ombrifuge of sorrow. Is controlling someone else's thoughts, hence behaviour, hence emotions unethical- the purest form of evil. Maybe. But what we know is not necessarily what is true. You soon will find out the difference between the two. Maybe. You soon will see that controlling is not owning, owning is not caring, caring is not loving, and loving is not. Maybe. Or you will call me a phony and throw these pages into the fire, so deliberately put on. Perhaps, because that is what we do. I want you to go to the next page to understand sensitivity of my approach.

You

There are two different yous:

The you

And

A you

The you wants you to be free and compassionless. A wooden block, floating in the sea of mortal constraints.

A you makes you laugh in a group or makes you gift your vulnerability and security

in exchange of trust and camaraderie.

The you is who you want to be when no one else would be.

A you is who you think others want you to be.

The you is lonely and desperate for escape.

A you lies to you that you are getting there or just having a bad day.

"Go out"

"Learn a new hobby"

"Call your friends"

He cries every time the you looks outside the window.

The you wants to write.

A you wonders whether others would like it.

The you has never cried.

It doesn't smile either.

A you did it last week.

With friends - for altruism,

Without - for loathing.

The you doesn't care if it hurt others

Care for them

Caress them

Burn them

A you, has to go to work tomorrow.

The you isn't any -ist

A you is as many -ists as it can to be

The you makes you starve yourself

Take an incense stick,

and forget the stab through your chest as you experience --

the high from an amalgam of

scent and suffering.

A you just ordered pizza.

The you is life and death

A you -- A moment.

Don't be the you.

You won't be able to be.

Don't be a you.

Why be?

Red

Four walls, covered in blood.

I take a knife and slice open my throat.

I reach to my heart and rip it out.

As it is still beating, I eat it.

Pain.

Eight walls, covered in blood.

I punch me.

I keep punching me until there is nothing left.

I cry.

Anger.

Twelve walls, covered in blood.

I take a shotgun and blow my brains out.

My face feels like a heavy flap, leaking blood all over the floor.

Rage.

Budding

Why does he cringe at photographs of friendships?

Why does he flinch on actions of affections? Is it the gestures?

No--The people

They all seem so-- ugly.

Literally

Floating buds of appalling yeast

"Hey bud, we all are one,"- said one of my hippie friends. Utterly unaware of its grotesque sense nonetheless.

Why does he want to vomit in himself?

When he sees the face of a blobfish, even in those who are closest to him.

He doesn't want this.

This--

Is hell.

Being repelled by his lovers. Disgusted by his friends.

Nauseated by their conversations.

Bunch of spores--

Living.

Time

.-.-.- -. .. .-- ....-.. .-.. .- ....-. .- -.. -. ..- --- -... ....
--- -. .... - .. .-- .... -.-. --- .-. .--. .... -.--
.-.. -. --- .... -.. -. .- .... --..-- -.- .-.. .- - .... ---
- .... -.-- .- .-- ....- .... -.-. ..- ... .
.-. . ...- --- .... -.. . --.. .. .-. .--. .... -... ....
--- - .... -.. . . -. ....-- --- .-.. ..-. ....-.
--- .... - .--. . -.-. -. --- -.-. .... -
....-.-.- - .. .. -.. -. .- .... --..-- ... . --..-- . --
.... -.-- .- ... . --- - .... -- ....-. --- ..-.
.... --. -. --- .-. .-- .... - .. ..-.-
.- ... -.. .-. --- .-- .... -. .. .. -.- -. .. .... - ....
--- - .... --..-- -.- -. .. .... - .... --- - ....
--. -. .. ..- .-. .-. .- -... -- . ... - .. ..-.-
.- -. --- ... .. .-. .--. ....- .... - ..-
--- .... - .. .-- .... -. .- -- ....- ....-. --- .... - ... --. -.
.- .... - ..- --- .... - .. .-- .... -. .- -- --- .-- ....-
.... --..-- -.. .- . .-. .... - .... - ..- --- .... - .. .-- .... - .. -.-
....- .... -.- .. .-.. ....-.-.- . ... -. . ... -....- -. --- -.
....-. .- .-.. ..- -.-. .-. .. -.-. .... -.
.. .- -- . .-. .... - .- .... - ....-.. .-.. .- ....-.-.- . ... -. . ... --- -. ....
... .- .... --..-- - -.-. . .--- -... --- .... --..-- -.. . ... ..- .-
-.-. .... - ....-.-.- --. -. .. -. .- . -- .... --- -. ....
- .... --..-- . -- .... --..-- - -.-. . .--- -... --- .... -
....-. .. .. -- .... -.-- -... .... -.. . ... ..- .- -.-. ....
- --- -. .... -.. . ... ..- .- -.-. .... - .- ....
.-- .... --. -. .. . -...

Woman

Once upon a time, in Auschwitz, there was a little boy named Gavriel Kazmerov. His hope was meagre and memories, weeping. His father left with a bunch of blonde adult people for work a couple of days ago. He missed him. But time was not left blank; the cruelty of humankind. He went on to his regular duties—sweeping and washing. Skies were as clear as the day permitted. He just kept swinging his broom around, brooming away the leaves from the Polish road.

"Hey, look where you are going," he accidentally ran into an old woman. She must have been in her fifties--her skin was wrinkly.

She looked at Gavriel.

Gavriel--quiet.

"I am sorry, miss."

She noticed an awful sadness in his eyes, a sadness which should not be present in the eyes of a five-year-old.

She knew the reason.

She knew why he didn't deserve it.

"You look like you are starving. Would you like some bread? I have a cottage nearby."

Gavriel was hesitant at first, but then he obliged. The woman walked a little funny as if she carried a lot of weight. All she wanted was to help this kid. And maybe, a little piece of bread with soup might help.

As they arrived at the cottage, Gavriel was happy to see the food.

"The last time I had such an amazing supper was with my father."

"Where's he now?" she instantly regretted that question. "I am sorry, but do not be sad. I have another present for you."

The thought of a present made Gavriel smile again. He loved presents. His father, a tradesman, used to bring exciting gifts whenever he would return from his trip. But all of that changed for poor Gavriel as soon as he was told he belonged to the rotten race.

"I think you will love this. It is for my special friend," she said as she took off all her clothes.

Gavriel was amazed. He had never seen a naked woman before; for him, this was all very fascinating.

"Come close to me, my little man."

She took his hand and gradually made him touch her. "This feels weird, miss."

She smiled. "It's okay. It feels good." She said as she gradually put his whole hand inside her.

Gavriel seemed delighted. For him, this was a game.

She gradually put his entire arm inside her, then his shoulder and then his head. Finally, she put all of Gavriel inside her. "This feels weird," said Gavriel, but he also felt warmth and comfort.

"It is okay, dear," said the woman as she returned to brooming the road.

It was a little breezy, which made the sky a little clearer. Times had been tough for everyone. But it will all be okay. At least, that is what she thought.

"Hey, look where you are going," a little girl accidentally ran into her.

"I am sorry, miss."

She noticed an awful sadness in her eyes. She knew she didn't deserve it.

"You look like you are starving.

Would you like some bread?

I have a cottage nearby."

Brunch

"Hey! How are you doing?"

As he imagined himself --being impaled by a pole passing through his mouth, tearing apart his rectum-- so that his maggot-infested stomach could be roasted over the fire-- because he feels like he deserves immense torment and suffering-- him wanting to be beaten to death with a hammer because that is what he feels represents the true nature of life-- his dead body being hung from the roof like a trophy-- covered in blood--his guts hanging out with his brains reeking of dog shit-- he said:

"I am doing great. What about you?"

Green

These lights are so beautiful

My face has no shape,

My feelings are there.

I know them.

I am disgusted by my body.

It has no borders.

It is fluid and randomly mixes with the air.

I want to fuck you.

I want our bodily fluids to flow through one another.

I want to drink your piss.

I want us to be gross.

Switch off the lights now.

Closer

She is still the same.

If not--better. I have never seen her this happy before--

We met a long time ago. It was a weird experience. We weren't in love at the moment. But yes, we bonded instantly. There has never been a soul. You know, in me. You know, then. But still, I was good at acting. And she might not have noticed that in time--hence, there we were having a great time. I felt connected, umm, to something, umm someone--after a long time.

But as time went, as it usually does, we oscillated between being friends and, well, whatever we were. But then, something happened. Between our individual sadness and loneliness--something triggered, and we grew closer together. We were there for each other's pain.

But that was a while back. It is different now. She has it all together, well now. I -- probably stayed where I was. It is great to see her-- like this. Her smile brightens the entire room. The shadows of our past, though, have gotten lost. Feels like I don't even know this person. If we would have met now, well then, no, we wouldn't have been friends.

So now, it is on me to make a choice--to stay in her life and unintentionally try to drag her down-- or to let her be. It's hard to love someone without letting them go.

Rules

No.

Here. Now.

Fear. Stress. Why?

We are.

Free. Lake.

Infimums.

Death.

Anyone.

No.

Here. Now.

Fall

When is it so?

Fuck off

Stop doing this to me!

Again

And Again

But suddenly, it stopped. There was nothing left but the purple vacuum.

But now-- Now I miss it.

I want it back

Even poison is loathed for by the thirsty.

Come back

Even though I know, it is not good for me

I want it

I crave it

I want it

Falling on my lips.

Grey

Every morning, you wake up--don't look into the colours of the mirror.

My identity is not there-- I … am not there.

They break me every single day. I get up.

I don't care.

They betray me, molest me, hurt me, shame me, kill me. I don't care.

They did make me, but I chose to ascend myself.

Retribution is a capital,

Society is a sin.

But all darkness is the nature of thinking.

And together, our blood is red enough to scare them. Our soul is purple enough.

They will not see me blue.

No matter what, we will wait until tomorrow.

Always.

About the Author

Stark is a freelance writer, philosopher, physicist, and art enthusiast. He believes in the rejection of language and logical structures in a Wittgensteinian sense to be able to peek at the nature of reality. He has struggled with chronic depression and suicidality since an early age and was only recently diagnosed with borderline personality disorder and PTSD. His mental health has left him with an innate sense of chaos and outsiderness. He is attempting to work through these while managing and attempting to do good science, art and philosophy, which in his opinion, are not much different.

CPSIA information can be obtained
at www.ICGtesting.com
Printed in the USA
LVHW031824070722
722894LV00003B/95

9 780228 863175